NOT-SO-FABLE
FABLES...

OTHER BOOKS BY
D.B. LICHTSTRAHL

ARE YOU WATCHING?
[Non-fiction]

NOT-SO-FABLE
FABLES...

D.B. Lichtstrahl

D.B. Lichtstrahl/LIGHTBEAM INFORMATION
Princeton, New Jersey 08542
dbl@humanidentity.net; www.humanidentity.net

A Case of Mistaken Identity! © 2012
A Sticky Story © 2012
Gazelle © 2012
Islands Next Door © 2012

ISBN-13 978-0-9777-844-3-1
ISBN-10 0977784436
FICTION - INSPIRATION - CONSCIOUSNESS - SELF HELP -
SPIRITUALITY - WELLNESS

EDITOR: Sharon Violet Sheiman
COVER DESIGN: Johanna Furst

Soft Cover
USA

IN ACKNOWLEDGEMENT OF

Our common core.

And, my sons Zach Isaac and Jacob Adam,
for assuring I remain in the lightness of.

BEFORE WORDS

What the caterpillar
calls the end of the world,
the master calls a
butterfly.
- *from Illusions by Richard Bach*

It's human to construct identity. Over time, identity arises (sometimes) without our awareness. As a "meaning-making-species" that seeks to understand what's all around, we humans absorb information and it becomes truth. It's only natural. Didn't we once believe the world was flat? And, at an even earlier time, that Earth was the center of an orbiting-planetary-system in the sky?

After a while, neither of those beliefs worked so well, and eventually they were known to be just plain inaccurate. It's the same with human identity. The body-first understanding (Earth as the center of the universe) has been swapped out for sentience, consciousness, core energy, the unified field,

Great Mystery, God, the substance that "turns us on"...(the Sun as the center). We are the act of watching—"perceiving happening" is the common core identity of Everything. Believing we are singular and separate from all that exists is now just plain inaccurate too.

Perhaps this new identity understanding is the Holy Grail humans have been questing for all along...

Playfully imagining and considering the "not-so-radical" —I bet hauntingly familiar, in fact—identity perspective presented within these pages is cause for celebration ...making any other understanding of who we believe we are now a case of mistaken identity!

I'm glad you're here.

D.B. Lichtstrahl
December 21, 2012

1
A Case of Mistaken Identity!
This tale unfolds the evolution of human identity, revealing its simple truth...

2
A Sticky Story
This is a tale of personal awakening...

3
Gazelle
This is a tale of relationship...

4
Islands Next Door
And this tale just is...

1
A Case of Mistaken Identity!

This tale unfolds the evolution of human identity,
revealing its simple truth...

Once upon a time...

Everything was alive...pulsating...
vibrating...expanding...experiencing
...playing.

A First Glance at Everything, and
you could see what Mattered...
tangible stuff like humans, creatures
of all kinds, plants and rocks and
water and such.

A Second Glance, with a squint of the eye, and it wasn't too hard to see the intangible stuff like human knowledge, and how that knowledge got shifted all around due to human imagination.

With a Third Glance and a slight tilt of the head, Everything appeared as one swarming, tiny particle soup, in perfect synchronization; Everything tangible and intangible, an ocean of quantum foam.

And...in a precise blink of an eye–at a Whole Glance–you were aware that you were *watching Everything,* the stuff that Mattered, intangible knowledge in all its arrangements

and the swarming particle soup.
From a Whole Glance, the view was
outstandingly divine.

Everything depended on the nature
of your Glance.

Everything, ever evolving, formed
perfectly into its even more beautiful
nature. Human knowledge accrued,
ideas arranged themselves, emotions
were stirred and all the fantastic
tangible bodies were inspired to
move (along with creatures of all
kinds, plants and rocks and water
and such).

Humans experienced what was all
around. They were on fire, running

about in an excitable kind of way. Mostly, they took to discovering things, and looked happily quizzical when aware of their differences. A good time was had by all.

As humans accrued more knowledge about Everything, they experienced their form as a kind of "boundary"... after all, it did move and shake, jump and run. It wasn't stationary, like a tree.

As far as they understood, their form wasn't "attached" to anything; and so evolved their body-first perspective of Everything. It was a First Glance only outlook.

From this body-first perspective they learned about the foods they preferred, where they lived, what to wear, and who to call friend. Because of this, Everything was understood as something "out there".

How their bodies moved and looked mattered most. Seeing only at First Glance did not afford them the opportunity to experience the wholeness of Everything.

And, not fully experiencing Everything they could, humans believed they were separate and different...from creatures...from nature, from one another...from *Everything!*

Over time, from their First Glance perspective, they learned about themselves from the "outside-in"... which they trusted. This presented a veritable feast of limited, unique perspectives. Some humans believed their limited perspective was best. Others walked away when that happened.

With this limited body-first approach shaping their experiences, they missed the Whole Glance. It just never occurred to them that much more might be happening beyond their fantastic, tangible bodies (and creatures of all kinds, plants and rocks and water and such) about which they knew so little.

After a while, an understanding of "*This is me, that's you*" formed, and humans attributed all they "did" to their bodies. Eventually, they gave a name to their understanding of "*This is me, that's you*" They called it their "Identity" or "I" for short. Everyone acquired an "Identity". Identities were like everything else "out there"—they were separate.

And so, a fantastic distortion grew...

Humans built bridges and constructed beach chairs. All were unique and useful. They attributed their creations to their "Identities" excitedly saying things like, *"I did this!"* and *"I did that!"*

They moved things around. So much so, that creatures of all kinds (maybe even plants and rocks and water and such) got annoyed.

Bothered by all the rearranging, the creatures of all kinds began showing aggressive behavior.
No one had ever seen that before.
Some of them disappeared. No one had ever seen *that* before either.

Humans, each with their own "Identity" wanted to create—and now collect—more stuff. This took up more room. Each human felt that their stuff was important, and being important, it now needed to be protected. "*This is me, that's you*" turned into "*This is mine, that's yours!*"

Pretty soon, emotions became charged and humans began arguing. Fists began waving with force and bodies flung on top of other bodies. This was nasty stuff.

Some humans experienced angry emotions and began saying things like "*Who do you think you are!!*"

Some experienced sad emotions and said things like " *Who am I?* " Some believed they were more separate than originally imagined and, believing that, they felt profoundly "alone".

With "Identities" in place, the fantastic distortion went unnoticed. Yet humans were not "separate" from Everything. And if separate was not who they were, they certainly were not...alone!

Between what Mattered, the intangible stuff, the swarming particle soup in perfect synchronization of which they were a part (including creatures of all kinds, plants and rocks and water and such) *and* their ability to observe at a Whole Glance, *humans couldn't have been more an aspect of one-synchronized-functioning-whole-Everything!* But who knew?!

A few humans embarked on a quest to find something they named "One-ness." They imagined in finding "One-ness" they'd be "enlightened" and would find their "True Identity" and their lives would change for the better.

Some began to search for their "One Soul-Mate"...another human. Those humans believed they were missing something and once they found their "One Soul-Mate," they would be "complete". Some kept searching, wandering about feeling like they didn't belong anywhere.

If you were observing *Everything*, you might think, "*Look at this...a bunch of humans with remarkable capabilities wandering around, sad, angry, lonely, arguing, moving things around, thinking "I" was their body ...searching, trying to belong...when even if they tried...they couldn't <u>not</u> belong!*" There existed only *one Everything, of which they were a part...* and it was simply divine!

Because humans believed their "Identity" to be " *This is me, that's you*" much destruction occurred (to themselves, creatures of all kinds, plants and rocks and water and such).

Replacing old knowledge with new, more accurate information was evolutionary. As more humans taught each other that their bodies were magnificent forms that were very much a part of Everything; when they started *watching* their unique intangible stuff and shared and received it with joy; and when looking with their heads slightly tilted at the swarming particle soup happened, (using tools they had built to watch it) repairing and healing began to happen, too.

Yet most important of all was *when they guided their young to watch.* This set into motion their wonderful capacity to experience a Whole Glance. This was truly divine advancement for *Everything;* and at the tipping point, the next generation of humans were the first to call Everything "I". They happily called themselves "Unique Points-of-View of the I". Their more evolved "I" perspective felt superbly spot-on, and over time they effortlessly looked out for one another...or rather, "Themself" (which of course *was Everything*).

Because watching felt so darned good, it became fundamental to the education of each Unique Point, in order for each to fully experience the wondrousness of Everything (and *watching* didn't take up any room, nor was there ever a shortage of it)! Ultimately, there was no longer a need to protect their stuff. "*This is mine, that's yours*" lost importance.

With this new *Everything-Identity*, war became obsolete. The nasty stuff stopped. Sure, humans got angry and fists waved radically at times, yet since there was no point in beating "Themself" up, the anger that occurred at each Unique Point expressed itself positively (which was a whole new way of experiencing

anger...which led to far less fear...
which led to magical sadness...and
way more joy...it's truly all
connected). Emotions became
delicious.

"I got *THIS* back!" one human
bellowed, instead of the old, "I got
YOUR back!"

By then they knew the only
imagined boundary "between them"
might be their diverse knowledge in
all its arrangements, which is why
" *This is me, that's you*" became,
" *This is 'my' unique intangible point
of view. And that's yours!*" (Yes it
was a mouthful–and somewhat
awkward at first, yet it felt so good

they went with it anyway!)

Encouraged by such a perfect understanding, one very young Unique Point-of-View popped up and shared...*"You could say Everything is like tentacles of the same octopus!"*

No one had ever heard *that* before.

An elder shouted with glee,
" Yeah...and if we are Everything alive, pulsating, vibrating, expanding, experiencing, playing...and there is only ONE-Everything, then we must be Everything experiencing itself from an infinite number of Unique Points-of-View including creatures

of all kinds, plants and rocks and water and such!"

" *Wow, wee!"* Everything roared in perfect synchronicity, *"...any other understanding must be a case of mistaken identity!"*

Once upon a time...

Everything was alive...pulsating... vibrating...expanding...experiencing ...playing...and *still is...*

– THE unEND –

2
A Sticky Story

This is a tale of personal awakening...

He was born...

the baby of four sons; golden hair and bright blue eyes, a spark of fire.
He was curious. A bundle of energy, observing what was all around.
He smiled a lot. He played a lot.
He had a direct line to the Akashic Field—*the stratum conveying all the information of Everything!*
He heard. He saw. He experienced.
He thrilled at looking at Everything.

When he looked, he experienced
a vibrational-wave of deliciousness.
He was all ears, eyes, nose, mouth,
sensation, and beyond!

Over time, as he evolved, he
experienced that which wasn't
a Vibrational-wave of deliciousness.
He didn't like the feeling of those
non-delicious experiences.
One might arrive in the form
of intense physical discomfort,
due to someone speaking in harsh
vibrational tones or waving a hand
at him with angry force. "Bad" was
the label given to such non-delicious
experience. A story had formed—
meaning made. It didn't read well,

sound good or feel welcoming...
this story. It wasn't beneficial in
any real way that occurred to him.
"Bad" was just plain...yuck. It came
from–he later understood–legacy
information learned over time.
It was passed down by guardians
to more guardians. As he grew he
didn't believe (because of how
much, "Bad" he experienced) that
his guardians were truly *guarding*
his vibrational-wave of deliciousness.

As a young man, he felt more as if
his guardians were "a bad joke!" as
by now, almost everything about his
story was "Bad".

Although he had delicious

experiences woven within
Everything now and then, with each
intensely uncomfortable experience
that arose, he smiled a little less and
played more quietly. (...Meaning
strings itself together, and quite
uniquely for each human.)

As time flew, his story got very
sticky. So sticky, he could barely
celebrate his delicious experiences,
like the Blue Lagoon during a
full moon with a Faerie Queen,
which usually brought him deep
exhilaration...delicious indeed!

His story was so sticky he could
barely see the parts–its separate
uniqueness–within a more

marvelous, entire story.

He could not look at it; hear it, taste it, smell it, nor feel his story because now, as an adult, he *was* his story; its meaning, interwoven, had absorbed him as its Main Character. Of course, delicious stories were experienced along the way, yet his story of "Bad" was the one that stuck most. He experienced it with far greater intensity and frequency than all the delicious ones (after all, he *was* the Main Character of *this* one). He looked around a lot less. He could feel its effects deep in his waters...in his bones.

He preferred the experiences that

arose divinely dream-like, when he looked at Everything; when he experienced *that* vibrational-wave (...of deliciousness); when his energy was on fire (right down to his waters)! When he experienced *that* story... "*Hey... Where did that one go?!*" he heard from a curious voice between his ears...and then...he was aware of hearing this...

"Books are stories we pick and read to be transported into the information there. Brains are like books, having been imprinted by experiences stored there in sentences, in audio, in Technicolor illustrations. The stories are strung together into a book named, "Me and My World." Imprinted, the information is noticed with each involuntary turn of the page; and images conjure themselves, naturally

fitting the body's expression. Sensing happens. Do I like what I notice? Do I like the feeling? The book, the hundreds of thousands of pages of data from which stories were shaped and meaning crafted, do I like it? Would I prefer another book with different stories...?"

To the right—his head tilted ever so slightly, all by itself.

In a moment's notice, he became aware that *he was "reading" his book*, the stories, in the thousands... of his own. He saw the pages turn ever so quickly- *"Do I even like many of the stories now?!"* he noticed. " *No!* " came the reply.

And then within a moment, he

noticed what he liked very much...
He liked the awareness of looking at his stories!

Experiencing *looking* was familiar and comfortable to him...in a brilliant sort of way.

A page turned to his childhood and he experienced smiling a lot and playing a lot. Shivers ran through his body and he grinned big.
He liked being aware of the book and its stories. It was expansive and sparkling to look...through it.
To look was an experience beyond the whole book of stories!

When *looking* he was no longer

only the Main Character. When looking he was the "Seer of the Page," which was accompanied by an infinite amount of deliciousness. He liked that a lot.

And in the moment of *noticing his book*, his stories unstuck themselves from "Bad" and, in a nanosecond, 99% of his non-delicious experiences recorded there—naturally re-strung themselves into the vibrational-wave he longed for!

In noticing the stories, his perspective had shifted from one of being the Main Character, to one of being the Producer, Director,

Cameraman, Script Writer, Sound-track Engineer, Narrator, *and* Main Character... *This felt way better! This was way more delicious!* " *This* was *that* experience I loved when I was young. I want *this* experience always!" The voice sounded loud and clear in the space between his ears.

And so organically, a sticky story dissolved into a vibrational-wave-of-delicious-human-experience within a more marvelous entire story, noticed in a book so large its joy could hardly be contained...and the uni-verse—including humans—flourished...

∞ NOW ∞

3
Gazelle
This is a tale of relationship...

Once upon a time...

there lived somewhere high in a mountain, deep in a cave, a lightning-slow Gazelle. She could leap huge pebbles while traversing the deepest puddle in search of all that was found.

One adventurous morning, while carefully selecting long tasty grasses, she looked up, paused and watched all that was familiar. Curiously, she

felt uncertain and Wobbled.
With so many years of peace and
satisfaction, she noticed this new
Wobble and the quiet questioning
that followed.

Unaccustomed to the Wobble,
she watched her whimsical leap
become a measured hike. All
that was vividly familiar turned
mundane, which caused her to feel
a bit droopy. So she trekked back
to the well-being of her cave.

At home, she found home to be
not-so-homey. She felt separate, and
in a peculiar way very singular. She
was concerned. She curled up in her
favorite spot and fell asleep.

While Gazelle dreamt, The Moon and The Stars talked among themselves and gazed upon her. They were happy when they radiated their essence over Gazelle, her plateau-topped mountains and rocky meadows. The Moon and The Stars knew Gazelle well and the abrupt Wobble she had felt in the early hours of light. They spoke about how they might support Gazelle going forth from her Wobble...or at least her cave. They wanted her to journey and experience her world more fully than she had ever known, with an even greater awareness of serenity and contentment than before.

"Where to begin?" imagined The Moon and The Stars. "*In The Middle!*" they howled joyfully, since it was in the Middle of Gazelle's life that she had felt the Wobble.

So far up high, deep into the Middle they went, looking for remedies they could offer Gazelle.

In The Middle was Everything-lost and Everything-found. In The Middle there were many, many, many more like themselves; Moons and Stars with unique light. They saw clusters among clusters, infinite groupings, galaxies, and conversations. Far enough, deep into the Middle, they followed the light until...just before the sun was due to rise, it dawned on them! Gazelle had no clusters! She had no groupings, no galaxies, or conversations!

They knew Gazelle was fond of leaping and laughing, skipping, dancing and loving. However, all that was beautiful and warm to Gazelle, all that was joyful and comfortable, she had accepted and used, and tasted, and eaten, alone.

The Moon and The Stars had found in The Middle, that in order to experience the fullness of joy, one must encounter clusters, groupings and Galaxies with which to share it!

For only when it is shared, is joy truly divine!

The Moon and the Stars were clear with their discovery, so they asked The Middle to whisper their new findings into Gazelle's inside ear. If their findings were not true to Gazelle—if the whisper was not heard—she would wake-up (not awaken) and feel a bit of a Wobble every now and then (for Wobbles are signs and don't really ever go away).

However, if their findings rang just right to Gazelle, she would open her eyes, throw caution to the wind and venture out in search of relations!

With bliss, she would share her stuff and receive great gifts in return...and feel the steadiness of joy!

It was now The Sun's turn to shine.

The Moon and The Stars were very pleased to see day happen, mostly because they were excited.

As the Sun's heat chilled Gazelle, The Moon and The Stars gazed into her cave wondering what would be.

And morning began...

Leaping to the mountaintop in search of clusters, groupings and

Galaxies ready to share her booty...Gazelle went forth!

The Moon reflected. The Stars glittered and The Sun was radiant.

≈ GOOD DAY ≈

4

Islands Next Door

And this tale just is...

We roam like Islands...

Alone,

   separate,

      independent,

different from the Island next door.

We work.

We play.

We feel the sun.

We feel distance from the Island next door.

We watch the stars and experience space.

We go to the edge and look out.

We wonder about the other close by.

We shout and hear ourselves.

We fall asleep aware of wave-sounds from deep waters.

We open our eyes and rise and walk.

Surprised, we wonder where the water has gone...

We watch our shores.

In the night they disappeared.

Without water surrounding us, what was not seen is revealed.

Curious, we journey from shore down into deep valleys.

At the deepest we stand still and look around in awe...

We see our Islands have disappeared...

In their place are mountains... mountains all around connected by endless, rich valleys in which we stand.

Standing where waters once existed we see connections.

And realize, connected we have always been, we are, and will always be.

And, even if we do not see,

we will always be,

not the Islands we thought we
were,

but mountains connected
evermore...

ΔΔ BEGIN ΔΔ

AFTER WORDS

Everything is a teacher pretending.
- from ARE YOU WATCHING? by D.B. Lichtstrahl

Not-so-fable fables sprang from the awareness that some might better understand what it means to be human through playful, made-up stories. Seems that's why fairy tales and other fantastical accounts have endured through time.

Whatever the meaning automatically conjured from these pages by each reader, may it enthusiastically offer a more useful point of view. More useful is always better—for everyone—when it comes to a point of view.

- D.B. Lichtstrahl

THANK YOU

The human catalyst for "dreamers" are the teachers
and encouragers that "dreamers" encounter
throughout their lives. They are invaluable in
the quest to turn ideas into reality.
– *Kevin Carroll Katalyst, Author*

From this Point of View (that would be mine...) there is no
such experience as one that is "alone". Therefore, I wish to
make known, my deeply-felt gratitude to Artist, Johanna
Furst for designing yet another outstanding book cover;
and to Sharon Violet Sheiman as Editor, once again
ensuring that the words strung together make as much sense
as possible. THANK YOU Josh W. Raymond maverick
extraordinaire who stirred the Gazelle in me, and to Robert
C. Lockwood who reflected back my sticky story.

Their excitement, creativity and generosity is contagious...
and that is good.

- D.B. Lichtstrahl

D.B. LICHTSTRAHL

The highest education is that
which does not merely give us information
but makes our life in harmony with all existence.
– Rabindranath Tagore

For more than 20 years, D. B. Lichtstrahl has been exploring and analyzing the art and science of communication and verbal expression. She has shaped branding and awareness campaigns for entrepreneurs and organizations, from noted financial institutions and software companies to non-profits and book publishers.

In her programs for adults and kids, she designs experiences to facilitate the unlocking of each individual's full potential for insight and innovation.

You are invited to continue exploring the human identity adventure at www.humanidentity.net.

On Twitter: @dblichtstrahl

On Facebook: Dana Lichtstrahl

On LinkedIn: Dana B. Lichtstrahl